KNUCKLEBALL

KNUCKLEBALL
BY TOM PITTS

"**Knuckleball** is a bruiser of a story that reads as fast as the title implies, and sits heavy in your mind long after you've read the last page. Pitts obviously knows the darkness of his city's gangland and portrayed here against the light of America's favorite pastime, while showing both sides their proper respect, is nothing short of remarkable. It's classic good and evil, hope and despair, but with Pitts, nothing is ever that cut and dry, and rarely does anyone get away clean. Conversational prose, brilliant ensemble casts, ratcheting tension, and the hint of something unexpected right over the next page is the reason to read Tom Pitts in the first place, but with **Knuckleball**, I'd say he knocked it out of the park. Top notch."
— **Brian Panowich**, author of *Bull Mountain*

"In **Knuckleball**, Tom Pitts finds the beating heart of San Francisco's Mission District, then reaches into its chest and rips that heart out. An ambitious and tightly-packed slice of modern crime fiction."
—**Jordan Harper**, author of *Love and Other Wounds*

"A gut-punch of a story written at a blistering pace by a master of street noir. If you dig tales with wire-tight tension, stuffed with characters that massage the margins of life then pick up Mr. Pitts latest work."
— **Mike McCrary**, author of *Remo Went Rogue*

"Tom Pitts' **Knuckleball** comes at you with all the twists and turns the name implies, a devastating snapshot of brutality and tragedy, rage and fear, and a twisted ray of something that almost passes for hope. Pitts deftly sets up lives you care about, then propels you forward as he knocks them down."
—**Jon McGoran**, author of *Drift* and *Deadout*

KNUCKLEBALL

a Novella

TOM PITTS

Published by **Shotgun Honey Books**

215 Loma Road
Charleston, WV 25314
www.ShotgunHoney.com

Cover Design by Bad Fido.

ISBN-10: 1-956957-33-2
ISBN-13: 978-1-956957-33-4

11 10 9 8 7 6 5 4 3   24 23 22 21 20 19 18

Dedicated to Patricia Phelps,
who, in her own way, allowed me
the time to write this novella.
We miss you, Pat.

KNUCKLEBALL

GAME ONE

HUGH PATTERSON WAS A COP. He was a good cop. That's all he ever wanted from his job, to be a good cop. When he was still at the academy a lot of the other cadets would talk about how long it would take them to climb the department's ladder after graduation. They had their eyes on higher ranks and higher salaries. Not Hugh, he was old school, a throwback to another era. He was concerned with justice, helping his community, helping old ladies across the street, and all that other stuff that seemed like a joke to the people of San Francisco. Save that stuff for the Boy Scouts, this is the real world, the Captain used to tell him. Hugh was not deterred. He was genetically predisposed to hardheadedness, passed directly from his father. He'd been teased plenty in high school; his skin was thick. He told himself that law enforcement was a higher calling. Do the right thing and follow it, even if your colleagues never hear the call.

Hugh loved his uniform, loved his beat. Twice a week he and his partner were required to walk the 24th Street corridor. *Only* twice a week, Hugh lamented. They would take their time strolling from General Hospital all the way to Guerrero Street, stopping to hand out SFPD stickers to kids, to tell the older men to pour out their beers, and to gather intelligence, what his dad had called street smarts. You have to know your beat, Hugh would tell his partner.

His partner, Alvarez, preferred the safety and swiftness of the prowl car. He thought Hugh was out of his mind. Too much walking, too many *Hello's* and *How ya doing's*. They weren't running for office for Christ's sakes. Officer Alvarez watched the drug dealers scatter as he and Patterson took their time strolling up the street. Anybody who was doing anything illegal on the street was gone by the time Patterson and Alvarez got there. Alvarez knew that Hugh's moral compass was sound, he just felt like they could make a few more collars if his partner was a little more aggressive about getting the jump on these little pricks out here.

The drug traffic on 24th Street ebbed and flowed, over time moving from block to block, but it never went away entirely. It was a fluid business that adapted easily. Up on 16th Street, the drug dealers were illegal aliens. Speaking no English and brand new to the USA, they were replaceable, popping up like the heads on a whack-a-mole game. Down on 24th, though, they were mostly second-generation Americans. All Hispanic, sure, but these were young guys who could speak English. They weren't in it to find a better life; they were in it to find *the* life. Just 'cause they want to be, don't underestimate them as wannabes, Hugh was fond of saying. Hugh's approach was to not grab the street dealers for small offences; possession, sales, and trafficking charges that would see them back on the same corner a few days later. He thought it was better to let the little ones slide and instead barter for a little intel. Hugh felt that if you had a better handle on the whole neighborhood, got a feel for the fabric of the place, if maybe you knew that street dealer's grand-mother perhaps, you stood a better chance of making a real dent in the street crime. You could develop a rapport of sorts, an understanding of what these guys were about.

Alvarez thought he was nuts.

"These kids are assholes, Hugh. I don't think they really give a shit about what their *abuelita* thinks, or what anybody thinks for that matter."

"They just act that way, partner. Everybody cares. *Everybody*. Trust me."

"You know what I think? I think you watch too many movies. You think Latin culture is all about the family, patriarch, matriarchs, all that bullshit. This ain't a movie, man. This is the Mission. They don't give a fuck about that shit, that's not what they're living day to day."

Hugh disagreed. He felt close to the people of the Mission. For the Hispanics, family was still important. It was important to Hugh, too. While he grew up, he watched the withering of the family unit in California and saw the rise of so-called San Francisco Family Values, but he wasn't swayed; he felt the core values would always remain, had to remain. The basic lessons his father taught him served him well at this job. They helped keep him grounded, helped keep his priorities in line, reminding him to see the big picture. That's why they walked the beat the way they did, to complete the circle, to acquaint themselves with the human side of the story.

There were plenty of victims who were just collateral damage, the family and friends who cared for the perpetrators. Beyond the pain of embarrassment, there were fines that loved ones had to pay, the missing incomes when the young and strong went to prison. There was also the clumsy snow-ball effect that unpaid fines and quick arrests had upon all the young men. They all had warrants. They were all waiting for the Man to show up and take someone away. Contact with the Man meant going to jail. A high hurdle of trust to overcome. Not too high, felt Officer Patterson. Might as well be the moon, thought Officer Alvarez.

Officer Vince Alvarez had graduated the Academy two years before Hugh. He loved his job as well, but liked to think he was a little more pragmatic about his approach. He did what he did to support his family. He loved his home life more than he ever could any job. To Vince, it was what was waiting for him at the end of the day that mattered: his wife. He'd met Sue in high school. She was Chinese, but her accent was the thickest Californian he'd ever heard. She was, by his estimation, the most beautiful girl he'd ever seen. Vince was determined to make sure *he* was the one who watched the girl become a woman and to be beside her to see her grow old. He was wary of possible threats of interruption from any side. He liked to think of himself as a family man, too, but to Vince, family meant Sue. He had no one else close by. His father, an alcoholic, had succumbed to cirrhosis years ago and his mother had gone to live with his own *abuelita* in L.A.

He and Sue lived together in the Sunset District not too far from where Sue had grown up and gone to elementary school. They enjoyed a life that was full of newlywed passion and they never talked about family plans. Having children was a subject that held a subtle taboo. Outwardly they both professed a desire for a family, but with each other the subject had never been broached. They were somehow afraid of jinxing their young love, that brief arc of passion that so many called the honeymoon phase—they were able to stretch that time, that feeling, from months into years. Now they both clung to each other, waiting for some outside force to thrust them into the next stage of their marriage.

Alvarez's plan was simple. Work your way up to a higher rank, then, with more dough coming in, work fewer hours. Spend more time with Sue. It was a little simplistic, but he followed his heart. Maybe with a little more security, a little more money, maybe then they could talk about kids. Vince didn't want to scare her off. He'd worked hard courting her in high school, worked hard getting her family to accept him, and he wasn't afraid to work hard to keep her.

* * *

Baseball brings spring to San Francisco. The winter rains peter out slowly and the wind never dies down, not really. The clearest indication of spring is the increased traffic South of Market for the day games at AT&T Park. There is a festive community feeling that creeps over the city and, before you know it, the rains have stopped completely and the summer has arrived.

In the Mission, it's hard to tell who's a gangbanger and who's not. The division between red and blue evaporates as everyone seems to be wearing Giants colors. Hats with the SF logo are worn from 16th Street to 24th Street. Hugh liked the neutrality. It made his job easier. Casual talk about the pitching squad and batting averages took the place of uncomfortable hellos. It was a conversation starter with young men who would have never otherwise opened their mouths.

Today was the first game of a three-game series against the Dodgers. The rivalry between the two teams went back generations, before Patterson was even born. Nothing banded Giants fans together like their hatred for the Los Angeles Dodgers. Orange and black "Beat LA" placards went up in the windows of liquor stores and dry cleaners. "Fuck LA" T-shirts were hot sellers among the sidewalk vendors on Mission Street.

It was mid-morning and Hugh could tell that many of the people filling the sidewalks with black and orange were heading to the park. First pitch was at one-fifteen that afternoon. Their shift was over at three. He hoped he could watch the end of the game at the taqueria across the street from the Mission station. Burritos, beer, and baseball. As near to nirvana as Hugh could ever get.

"It's the three Bees, Vince. How often do we get to enjoy them together?"

"About twice a week," Alvarez said.

"Yeah, but do we take advantage? The opportunity knocks but we don't answer the door. C'mon, for ol' time's sake, let's watch the boys do in the Dodgers."

Alvarez didn't answer back. He knew better than to try to explain himself to Hugh. He'd let the subject alone until it inevitability resurfaced a few minutes later. Hugh could ask all he wanted, but Alvarez was not going to join him. It wasn't that he didn't care about the game; he just hoped to catch the last innings at home with his wife. Alvarez was a loyal Giants fan, but he'd heard enough about the game today from his partner and the people on the street. He'd listened to the opinions of scumbags and perps, shopkeepers and mailmen, delivery drivers and barbers, and from just about anyone else that his partner could elicit a comment. The only thing that kept his partner from talking to every single person they passed was Hugh's inability to speak Spanish. He understood the language slightly better than he could speak it, but it was a constant barrier between Hugh and the denizens of his beat.

"*Hola*," Hugh would say, making a swinging motion with an imaginary bat, and then he'd say, "*Gigantes*." Almost without exception, the only looks returned to him were confused. Hugh would continue on with an almost religious zeal, ignoring any embarrassment that Alvarez might be feeling. Perplexed immigrants would look to Alvarez for clarification, wondering if the elaborate pantomime might be something more sinister.

That was one of the reasons Hugh liked 24th Street best. The young men in *the life* down on 24th had sat in

American schools. They were a little less apprehensive, and could make small talk a little easier.

Miguel Martinez was one of these young men. On this morning he was walking down Capp Street for one reason, to avoid bumping into anyone. Especially cops. Capp Street was a half-block off busy Mission Street, away from most of the hustle and bustle and familiar faces of the neighborhood.

Hugh knew Miguel by sight, was pretty sure he knew his name too. One of the many young neighborhood gangbangers who did their best to slide by Hugh without notice. In the past he'd been unapproachable, but today Hugh saw his opening.

"Gonna finish 'em off today, huh?"

Miguel wasn't sure if he heard the cop right. The Giants were the furthest thing from his mind. Miguel didn't give a shit about the game. He was focused. He had two ounces of raw crystal meth sealed tight in his jacket pocket and a snub-nosed .38 stuffed into his waistband at the small of his back. Miguel froze. He didn't say a word, didn't smile, didn't nod.

Hugh realized he'd caught the young man off guard. Perhaps the kid was just stoned. Apprehension was natural when talking to the cops. Hugh knew it, and forgave it.

"The Dodgers," Hugh said.

Miguel still didn't respond. Hugh nodded toward Miguel's chest. Miguel looked down and saw the

Giants logo. He'd forgotten grabbing the shirt off the floor when he dressed that morning.

"Oh, yeah. Fuck them." Miguel still hadn't moved.

Hugh took another step toward him. Alvarez stood still and silent, too.

"Your name is Miguel, right?" Hugh said. "You have a little brother named Philippe?"

Miguel didn't answer. He didn't like cops, even friendly cops—especially friendly cops. Answering these simple questions felt like cooperating to Miguel. The cop seemed to already know the answers to his questions; Miguel felt they may be a trick. To answer might lead him to give up something, open a door for this cop to walk right through.

"You live with your grandmother over on 21st Street, right?"

"Right," was all Miguel could manage. The speed was triple-wrapped in his pocket and felt bulky and conspicuous. He imagined the gun slipping right through his waistband and falling heavy to the sidewalk. He tried to keep an eye on the other cop, the quiet brown one looking like he was ready to draw.

Hugh could see the kid was nervous. He figured it was all that weed these kids were smoking. It made them paranoid, unsociable, and slow-witted.

"Sanchez is starting 'cause Lincecum is on the disabled list. Should be a good one. You going?"

"Fuck no."

The comment closed the conversation. Hugh had reached out and that was enough for one day. He and Miguel would see each other again and would build their relationship one difficult conversation at a time. Hugh nodded. It was a tacit excusal.

Miguel breathed a sigh of relief, but stayed frozen till the two cops began to walk farther down the block.

"Pricks," he whispered at their backs.

• • •

Oscar Flores hated his brother. He knew it may even be a sin, to hate your own brother the way he did, but the way he saw things, it could be no worse than the sins his brother committed. This way, it was a wash. Oscar hated Ramon from as far back as he could remember. He couldn't recall a warm moment shared between them. Ramon was a sadistic son of a bitch. Except his mom wasn't a bitch; she had to deal with Ramon, too.

Everyone in the neighborhood thought Ramon was a tough guy. Oscar knew better. He knew Ramon was a chicken-shit. He could remember when their father used to beat Ramon. First he'd have to catch Ramon, and then, when he began to administer the punishment, Ramon would flail and wail like an infant. Their father left seven years ago, when Oscar was eight years old. That was the last time Oscar heard Ramon cry.

Oscar worked hard to avoid his older brother. He came home late, went to bed early, avoided the kitchen, and was quick in the bathroom. He still spent time with his mother, but if Ramon was home, he avoided her too. Any possibility of intersecting with his brother brought anxiety to Oscar, stress that had recently started to manifest with dozens of pimples across his oily forehead.

Oscar wanted to be left alone. The abuse he took from his brother only confirmed what he'd known all along; the world had only pain to offer. He watched his mother work endless hours just to come home to complain that there was never enough; never enough hours to fill her paycheck, never enough money from her paycheck, and never ever enough hours in the day.

For her part, Ria Flores never understood the animosity her boys shared, could never grasp her role in their relationship. Brothers fought, she knew that. Ramon always had a wild streak. It was only natural. She worked hard as a salon manager and knew that the long hours took a toll on her family. But it was a compromise; hard work without a husband, or a miserable life of leisure with plenty of extra time to fight, plenty of time to play detective and discover your husband's hobbies, plenty of down-time to apply make-up to those bruises.

At fifteen, Oscar Flores's life consisted of school, video games, and hiding from his brother. And baseball. Oscar learned to love baseball while hiding from Ramon. He spent long afternoons in his room watching games on his TV with the volume turned way down. Fate was smiling on Oscar and the Giants for this series. He knew it. There was no school that day and, as far as he was concerned, that was because of the series. He sat patiently in his room waiting all morning for the first pitch at one o'clock. He felt a connection between the dusty shafts of light that filtered into his room and the bright, wide-open sunshine bleaching the fans down at AT&T Park. The same wind that whipped though the bleachers at the ballpark rolled across San Francisco, channeled through the hills and then, moving easily over the flat Mission, blew through the open window above his head. On those days, he was no longer in his room; he was out there with his people. To one day be a ballplayer was a far-fetched fleeting fantasy for Oscar, but to be there at the park, with the fans, that was a reachable dream, a possible reality—practically true. Up in the box with the announcers, in line at the concession stands, sharing opinions with the stranger next to him, these were the things he could and would do. There was a warm feeling inside of him when he watched those games, especially those day games. It was a feeling of family.

Nothing brought family together like prayer. And on this day they were all praying for an end to the top of the sixth inning. The Giants had been up two runs for most of the game, but now the Dodgers had runners on second and third and the winning run was at the plate. Sanchez, who'd been on the mound all day, was showing signs of wear. Oscar felt as though he'd pitched the game with him. He hadn't gone to the bathroom or the kitchen since the game began. He was afraid now that any absence from the screen might be noticed, marked by karma, or luck, or the great God that controlled baseball, and the lead—with one solid crack of the bat—would be gone.

The pitcher wound up.

The bedroom door opened just a crack.

"Fuck you doing, faggot?"

Oscar didn't say a thing. He kept his eyes focused on the TV in front of him, watching the pitch. *Strike one.*

"Hey, you fucking bitch, you got ears?"

Oscar's focus was intense. He was willing himself to the park. He was the ball boy on the green, waiting. Another wind up. *Ball one.* Ramon began to look around the room for some imagined object, flipping over empty plates and DVD's and games cases. Oscar could smell the malt liquor on his breath. The faint smell of beer and stale cigarettes permeated the room. Oscar tried his best to stay at the game, to be invisible. *Strike two.*

The first punch jolted him. A square blow to the back of the head. He expected it, yet it always surprised him. Just for a second, everything went white. He could hear Ramon's sick chuckle. *Ball two.* The next one landed on his ear. Ramon's breathing sounded tinny and far away, but Oscar could feel his hot breath near him. It was the game that was distant now. The park, the people, were all now strangers. Cold and ignoring.

"Hold still, you piece of shit."

• • •

Hugh Patterson stood in front of a taqueria at 24th and Capp. The game played silently inside while Hugh stood transfixed. Sanchez wound up, threw, and crack, a double. Both runners on base made it in. A collective moan went up all over the neighborhood. Except for Hugh. A small smile crept across his face. He loved the tension. That's what made it a real ball game. There was never any worry for him, not really. It was a matter of faith. He didn't think there was any chance of the Giants not pulling it off.

"Eh, I gotta make a phone call."

He'd forgotten Alvarez was even there. Hugh nodded and returned his attention to the game. They both carried mobile phones; he couldn't understand why Vince felt the need to walk away every time he needed to make a call. "Go, go. I'll be right here."

Alvarez longed for the privacy of a phone booth. He didn't want anyone hearing the conversations between him and his wife. Any chance he could, he'd find the most secluded corner possible, turn his head toward the wall and, with an index finger stuck in one ear and the phone clamped onto the other, make his call.

Vince dialed home and got no answer. It was the middle of the afternoon, where the hell could she be? He dialed again. His heart skipped a beat. Was she ignoring his calls? Was she somewhere where she couldn't answer the phone? Was she afraid for him to know where she was? Or was she with someone and she didn't want him to know?

He tried to counter these thoughts, but they came too fast. He'd always rationalized his way around these things, finding a way to quiet the jealous voice inside his head. He knew if he could just hear her voice then it would be fine, *he* would be fine. He walked up 24th Street, staring into his phone and redialing.

Third time is a charm. She picked up.

"Baby, where you been?"

Behind Alvarez, there was a crack. Not the crack of a ball against a bat, but the loud, flat crack of a gunshot.

It only took one bullet to put down Officer Hugh Patterson. It was unnecessary to pump an extra four into his head. The blood flow from a wound like that—when the head is opened up while the heart is still beating—is enormous. It was flowing so fast that the puddle of blood had a ripple. It snaked down toward the gutter, slick and almost black. He lay there, still, not a shudder, not a chance. There was brain matter and skull fragments yards away. An explosion of blood and hair. For the last shot, the killer had bent down and put the gun under Hugh's chin, turning the top of his head into a volcano.

There were screams long before there were sirens, but the neighborhood was still slow to walk out to investigate. The five shots turned curious heads at the Wells Fargo ATM line at 23rd and Mission, a half a block away. None of them turned quickly enough to get a good look at the dark figure sprinting away. They stepped out into the street to look, but not too fast, they knew this neighborhood. Stray bullets and getaway cars were always a risk. A block away, at 22nd and Capp, several tough looking *hombres* ran out of the El Trebol bar in defense, clutching the guns in their waistbands and jackets and shouting to one another in Spanish. The gang that couldn't shoot straight. Drunk and blinded by daylight, they saw no shooter, no victim. The coast was clear.

Alvarez heard the shots and froze.

"Fuck."

He didn't bother to hang up the phone, he just turned and ran.

"Fuck."

When he didn't see Patterson in front of the taqueria, he figured that his partner must already be running to the scene. Where the fuck was the scene? Alvarez didn't radio in, he just ran.

By the time he reached the corner of 24th and Capp,

he could hear civilians wailing. Near the corner of 23rd, there was a cluster of people. They were knotted together with their backs turned to him. He started up Capp Street, scanning the onlookers for Patterson. Still not hearing anything on the radio, he keyed the mic and said, *"Thirty-oh, ten-seventy-one, ten-seventy-one. Shots fired. Shots fired. 23rd and Capp."* He was out of breath. Where the fuck was Patterson?

It was quickly apparent there was a victim. The onlookers were circled around a body. Most of them had cell phones in their hands, either taking pictures or already on the phone with 911. A woman turned away to retch and the group opened up. Alvarez peered in and saw the blue uniform first. Is that blue? Yes, it's blue. Another cop? A security guard, maybe? His mind, always rationalizing. Lying to him.

An older woman with wet eyes turned to him and said, *"Llamar a la policía."*

The police? He was the police. He squinted at her, trying to read her lips. She was still speaking, but Alvarez could no longer hear anything.

Where the fuck was Hugh?

"Fuck."

This time the word sounded like it had been punched out of him. It was barely a whisper. All the heads in the circle turned toward him, waiting to see what he would do. What was he going to do about one of his own? Vince's mouth began to water. He tasted bile. He kept wanting to make a positive ID, wanting to see the face, confirm it was not Hugh. He couldn't find it. There was no face. He saw tufts of red hair glued with blood to everything. He saw the little gold SF Giants logo that was pinned to the uniform, not permitted by regulation. But where was the face?

"Thirty-oh? Thirty-oh?" Alvarez's radio chimed in stereo with his partner's.

• • •

The **San Francisco Chronicle**'s headline read *Shot Down!* The *SF Examiner*'s headline simply read, *Blood-Bath* in letters so fat the word had to be broken in two. Local morning news shows all claimed to have exclusive story information. On Muni buses, in Starbucks lines across the city, people on their way to work traded opinions about the scumbag who gunned down the police department's most positive force. That's what the paper called Patterson. Overnight, he'd gone from being a happy-go-lucky guy floating by on dumb luck to being canonized as a true hero of the city, a throwback to the white-hat mavericks of the Wild West.

Oscar folded back the first section of the *Chronicle* and turned directly to the sports page. The Giants 5-4 loss to the Dodgers yesterday seemed perfectly in tune with the sour mood that hung over the whole city.

There were crime scene detectives and uniform cops crawling over every inch of the corner below their apartment last night. He watched them from the window in his room, keeping his TV off so he could overhear their police banter. Bits and pieces of information came in clips. It was English but sounded as foreign to him as Chinese. It went on through the night. The police radio was the lullaby that had put him to sleep. He was tired of thinking about it.

Oscar's mother puttered dutifully around the kitchen. Motherly multi-tasking: putting away dishes, pouring cereal, wiping the stove, making lists. Her deliberate menial tasks took on an insect-like business quality. It blocked out the chaos of last night. His mother didn't mention a word about the shooting, even though police came to interview her four different times during the night. Oscar watched her scrub and organize as though it warded away evil spirits.

"Come on, Oscar, hurry up and finish your breakfast," she said for no real reason at all. It was Saturday; there was no school for him and she didn't start work at the hair salon till ten.

Ramon had been gone most of the night. He left late and then stayed gone. When he saw his chance to get out, he took it. When the doorbell rang at midnight, he was sure to slip out behind Ria Flores as the detectives were asking their questions. He knew that a young Latino man would be less scrutinized exiting his own house with his mother beside him. He kissed her on the cheek and said he'd be home in an hour. He was down the last few steps and almost to the street before the cop was able to ask him to wait.

The detective asked him a few quick ones, "How tall are you? When were you born? Where were you born?" Simple fast ones, a barometer of guilt. Nerve check.

Ramon was used to it. He knew how it worked. He gave direct, basic answers, saying close to nothing but speeding the interview along.

Ria stepped in, voiced her disapproval, added weight to his alibi. After all, he was inside at the time of the shooting, she said. It was the truth. The same truth she repeated to the detectives until the early morning hours.

"I want you to gather all those clothes on your floor and put them in the basket. That's why we got it, to keep the clothes off the floor." Ria spoke to Oscar without looking at him.

Oscar sat at the table letting his cereal get soggy, staring at the picture of Sanchez on the mound. Sanchez had his head down. He looked as disgusted as the city felt.

Beyond disgust, the city felt outrage. There was talk of illegal aliens, youth crime, mandatory minimums, stricter gun laws. There needed to be a special unit to find the killer. A ten thousand dollar reward was announced by the SFPD. The Commissioner promised the department would not rest until there was justice. Flags were lowered to half-mast.

When word filtered out that the killer was most likely a young Latino male, *Oakland Tribune* columnist Mitch Tatum jumped the gun and called the killer "a scourge that vilified all hardworking, honest Latinos trying to overcome racial bias." The culprit was demonized to become larger than life. The story eclipsed all others. By two o'clock that day the reward was raised to fifteen thousand. By five o'clock the SFFD kicked in another ten, with Chief Buchwald stating that "no one in a uniform was entirely safe if someone such as the killer were to be allowed to walk the streets." And by the time that Oscar was trying to ignore the news, the reward was up to thirty thousand dollars.

• • •

Vince Alvarez sat on his brand new weight bench with his head in his hands. The cold steel of the weights around him seemed to reflect his mood. He'd been home only an hour. The morning light streamed through the curtains, the stillness making his happy home seem more like a mausoleum. The night had been filled with endless interviews at Hall of Justice. Endless paperwork. The same questions over and over. He was exhausted, wrung out.

Sue paced, lightly as a cat, working her way back and forth in front of Vince. She wanted to approach him, ask questions, comfort him at least. She could only tiptoe back and forth with her hand clenched over her mouth, holding back those questions like a cough or a sneeze, something that nature was trying to force out.

"I shouldn't have left him," Vince said. He held his head in his hands and stared straight at the carpet.

"You said he was watching the game, right? What could have made him walk away from that?"

"No shit. Fuckin' jerk. He was glued, too, standing there with that stupid grin on his face. I didn't think he'd walk away from the game, not for anything." Vince paused and looked up at his wife. "He said he wasn't going anywhere. I'll be right here, that's what he said."

"It's not your fault, you know."

There was a long unhealthy pause while Vince let this sink in.

"I know. I know it's not my fucking fault. Why would you even say that? I mean, what the fuck? Do you think it's my fault?"

"No, no." She was sorry she opened her mouth. "No, honey, no. I didn't mean that at all." She took a step toward him, reached out, but didn't touch him. His head went back into his hands. And the morning crept on.

The Police Officers Association had counsel for Alvarez within hours, the in-house guy they used for everything. Then the department's interviews turned decidedly more aggressive. His adversaries were now accusers. As soon as he lawyered up, his position, as far as they were concerned, became solidified; there was something he was hiding. Alvarez felt like a pariah.

It was police policy that he be put on administrative leave. As it was any time an officer involved shooting occurred, whether he fired his weapon or not. Last night, the POA lawyer told him not to worry; that, technically, he wasn't involved in the shooting. It didn't put Vince's mind at ease, not for one second.

"I'm a cop." Alvarez reminded him. "Don't blow sunshine up my ass. Tell me what the fuck is going on."

"Vince, do you mind if I call you Vince? Vince, try not to worry. The department has to go through its procedures, you know this. I'm just here to help guide you through it. Just try to relax and keep your head clear. Answer the questions honestly and we'll take it from there." The attorney—*his attorney*—smiled at him, his words whistling a little through the large gap between his front teeth. He wore thick glasses that made him look academic, but Vince couldn't shake the feeling that the guy was just an old cop who couldn't hack it on the streets.

Now, back in his own home, he could sense Sue's support eroding. She was upset that some action of her husband had now upended their life. Some fuck-up, some avoidable mistake of his, like forgetting to take out the garbage or pay a credit card bill. She couldn't understand. The phone calls he made were to her, yet she couldn't understand. How could she? How could he tell her that he trusted her so little that an unanswered phone could mean infidelity? Those phone calls amounted to an accusation. Truth was, if she had not answered that third call, he would have left his beat, his partner, sped straight to their Sunset home and stormed in to catch her in the act. What act? He didn't know; she'd answered the third call.

"Now what?" Sue asked. She didn't want to ask, but she couldn't take standing in the silence anymore.

Vince lifted up his head from his hands and looked at his wife through bloodshot eyes and said nothing.

• • •

"You see that shit yesterday?"

"I heard it, didn't see shit." Ramon knew better. He didn't know who capped the cop or why. Knowledge can be a dangerous thing.

"Cops is still everywhere, man."

"Talking shit."

"Provoking shit."

"Exactly," Ramon agreed. He and his friend, Salty, were sitting on a small side street off of 24th. They sat warming themselves on some dirty marble stairs, sunshine barely overpowering the wind. They shared a beer wrapped in a stained brown bag that was plucked from the gutter. They picked the bag up because the beer was stolen. 24-oz. Budweiser in a can. Salty joked that he stole so much beer from that same corner store he should be asking for a bag anyway. Ramon hated Budweiser. It tasted like piss but that was all Salty could get his hands on.

Fuckin' Salty. Snaky be more like it.

Ramon's standards were never high when it came to companionship; he deemed those same standards a necessary quality in his friends as well.

Ramon and Salty had known each other since first grade. Together they did palm cuts, cigarette burns, pissing contests—actual pissing contests—first blunts, first boosts, first arrests. Ramon had known Salty before he was known as Salty. Ramon knew why he was called Salty and helped him keep it mysterious.

"Fuckin' unbelievable. Crazy balls, man. That's what they should call that guy. Crazy Balls."

"Who?"

"The guy. The fuckin' guy who did this, man. Shoot a cop in the middle of Capp Street. Fuckin' crazy."

"Shit," Ramon said. The beer wasn't even halfway done and it was already flat. Ramon thought it took more than crazy balls to do something like that. It took something evil. All that blood. Leaning over. Sticking a gun under the cop's chin.

"Ramon?" Salty said. Ramon wasn't listening. He was staring at the cement between his shoes. "Ramon, what you got going today? You still got to do shit for your moms or are we free to party?" Salty tried to make it sound upbeat like a rhyme. To party meant doing what they were doing right now. On these steps or maybe they would move to a different spot. A blunt, some more beer if Salty could steal it with out fucking up, wait for someone else to show up with another blunt, bullshit, bullshit some more.

"No, I ain't hanging. Fuck that. All these fucking cops jacking everybody up. I'm going home to watch cartoons." It was true; he didn't want to answer any more questions. Cops scared the shit out of him. But more than anything he wanted to get off the street. He was sick of looking at that sidewalk, the gutter. The grey, lifeless color of it. All that blood. The guy with the hood, leaning over.

"Hey, you see that game yesterday? Fucking Dodgers."

"Salty, what the fuck do I care about the fucking Giants? I look like a big baseball fan to you?" Ramon handed the beer back to Salty. "This shit tastes like piss."

Ramon stood up and walked away without saying goodbye.

"Nice shirt, dickhead." Salty called out.

Ramon looked down and realized he hadn't changed his shirt since the day before.

He was still wearing Oscar's Giants shirt. Fuckin' Salty.

GAME TWO

WHEN THE GIANTS faced the Dodgers again that night there was a somber moment of silence before the start of the game. Thoughts and prayers went out to the family and friends of Officer Hugh Patterson as his cadet graduation picture loomed giant across the scoreboard. His smiling face, full of blind faith and stubborn optimism, looked impossibly young and possibly immortal when stretched to nearly sixty feet. When the announcer told the crowd that Hugh was a tireless Giants booster they hooted and hollered. It was infectious. A slow roar built up, the crowd adjusting to cheering for a dead man.

It was game two of the series today. First pitch at 7:15 pm. Oscar hated the night games on a Saturday. It meant he had to wait all day to watch the game. He tuned in early and saw the spectacle unfold under Patterson's image. He'd seen the cop around the neighborhood. He had never spoken with him, had not known that he was a Giants fan either. Seeing his face on the screen, Oscar thought Hugh looked like a Giants fan. His face, he thought, looked like baseball itself, as though the face on the jumbotron was staring back at him from an old bubblegum card. It was only missing a nickname like Shoeless or Boomer or Dusty. Oscar thought Hugh looked like what a *real* American should look like: Apple pie. Hugh's face didn't make Oscar think of San Francisco, it made him think of clean-sounding places he'd never been with names like Utah and Ohio. Oscar contemplated that face and felt a little sick.

Oscar tired to forget about the face, but every time the game broke to commercial there would be a quick fifteen-second teaser for the evening news. There the face would appear again. Hugh's face, staring back at him, spliced between shots of his street corner and the anchorwoman with a police shield superimposed behind her head. Oscar checked for his bedroom window in the shots from 23rd Street. His house looked so strange on TV. It was hard to recognize their front door. The whole block appeared strange to him. A little cartoony. Invented like a movie set, a sound stage.

He stood up and peeked out the window wanting to see the street for himself, check the corner and compare to the one on the television. There were white vans and bright lights out there still. There were two different reporters talking at the same time. Two cameramen filming. Two sets of bright white lights washed the normalcy away. Oscar thought the corner outside his window looked fake too, just like the one on TV. Not real, not the corner he knew. Nothing like yesterday. That's what the cameras wanted to show. The blood. That's what everyone wanted to see. All that blood.

• • •

Vince was sitting on a folding chair at a bare table in an interview room. He was on the opposite side from where he was used to sitting. He sat alone with the door open, familiar cop-shop sounds echoing down the hall. He could hear the ballgame on someone's radio, guys bullshitting, gruff testosterone-fueled cop talk. And laughter.

A tall, nondescript man came in and closed the door. He wore the uniform of the office cop, white shirt, dress pants, polished black shoes. It was the same detective that interviewed him yesterday, Detective Terry Schmitz. He looked at Vince and smiled. Or maybe he winced.

"I understand you gave some preliminary statements last night. Now we just wanna nail down a few spots, here and there. After all, we gotta hurry up and get this son of a bitch, right?"

Preliminary? He gave six hours of interviews well into this morning. He said nothing to Schmitz. Alvarez tried to play back the answers he gave last night. He had told the truth. Almost. He had to stretch a little. He couldn't face the fact that he was so far away when the shots were fired.

"How ya feeling, Vince? Did you get any rest? Can I get you anything before we start?" The detective didn't wait for any answers. He sat across from Vince and flipped open a yellow legal pad, wet a pencil on his tongue, and started where they had left off.

"So when you got to the block."

"On to Capp Street?"

"Yeah, Capp. When you hit the block, you said you may have seen a figure."

"It may have been him."

"The shooter?"

"I dunno. I saw someone."

Terry wrote something down and continued.

"You running top speed?"

"Not all the way. I had to exercise some caution."

Schmitz took a moment and adjusted his wrist-watch. "Because you saw the perp."

"Because I heard the shots."

"You heard the shots when you hit Capp Street?"

"No, before I was on Capp."

Schmitz took his perfectly sharpened pencil and made a notation on the yellow legal pad. "On the corner?"

"Yes. On the corner."

"All five shots?"

"All five shots."

"Let's go over again where you were when you heard the first shot."

And so it went.

At AT&T Park that night a small force of volunteers walked throughout the concourse with black and orange buckets taking donations for Patterson's family. During the fifth inning, with no fanfare and with no context to the game, it was announced that the reward had been raised to thirty-five thousand dollars. A cheer of support went up and the picture of Hugh was once again splayed across the jumbotron.

This all played out on local television, and during the commercial break the TV news showed a sketch of the shooter. A male Latino, approximately 5'10", 160 lbs, black hoodie, blue jeans, last seen running east on 23rd Street at South Van Ness, 2:35 pm Friday afternoon. The sketch was a caricature of no one. It was the same fractured facial composite charcoal drawings that go out to the public after any crime of this magnitude. As anonymous as a blank page.

Down the hall from where Vince Alvarez was being interviewed, Bobby Reese sat at a table identical to

Alvarez's. Bobby leaned forward, straining to hear the game through the open door. The noise in the police station drowned out the nuances of the play-by-play, but he managed to catch the score and the inning, Giants 3—1, top of the fifth. The volume jumped at the commercial and Bobby listened to the shooter's description with the rest of San Francisco.

Detective Schmitz walked in and closed the door. He stood looking at Bobby. He nodded his head a little, like maybe he knew something Bobby didn't know.

"Bobby," he said. Like it was a greeting, as though they were old friends. "Bobby Reese. Bobby Reese." The detective repeated his name, trying it on for size, hearing how it sounded. "I thought you maybe looked kinda familiar, and now that I'm looking at your sheet here, I see why. Geez, Bobby, maybe we ought to ask you to chip in for rent around here, you seem to spend enough time."

"Why Latino?" was all Bobby said.

"Excuse me?"

"*La-ti-no*. Why you all think this guy is Latino. I just heard the thing on the news. They say they looking for a Latino."

"Yes." Unraveling information from an interviewee was a subtle business. Detective Terry Schmitz liked to use the technique he borrowed from television psychologists, a lot of tacit agreement and the occasional, *How does that make you feel?* The person usually just wanted to unload, wanted someone to listen. They wanted someone in a position of authority to hear them—and agree with them.

"How you know a guy is Latino—with a hood on? How brown was he? Sure he wasn't one of them terrorist motherfuckers from Afghanistan?"

Terry smiled at Bobby and raised his eyebrows a little to let Bobby know that he got the joke but he was waiting for the punch-line.

"Guy I saw?" Bobby continued, "Couldn't tell. Not for real. Not for swearing to. You could presume, maybe. You could presume that this little fuck was a Latino. I mean, I did—I still do, but he wasn't flying no colors and I didn't axe to see no green card."

Bobby thought that was hilarious.

"No colors?"

"No colors."

"This is 23rd Street. No colors, huh? Bobby, you know those guys down there, don't you?"

"I maybe know some, you know, the ones who deal." Bobby also thought this was hilarious. He paused to let the Detective chuckle or respond. Schmitz was quiet, but offered up a little smile.

"It wasn't none of them guys, none of them guys I know."

"What about 18th Street? How about one of those guys?"

"How the fuck would I know, I could barely see the guy and he wasn't wearing no colors."

"All in black. Like the grim reaper."

"No, man, like I told your man over there, jeans, some baggy shit, black hoodie and a Giants t-shirt, you know, just the logo, the old-school one with the ball. Shoes? I didn't notice no shoes, I never do. I already told the other guy all this shit."

"I'm not talking to him, I'm talking to you. You tell me what *you* saw so I can understand. If you can make it clear to me, make me see what you saw, we won't have to keep asking you the same damn questions all day. Now, let's start at the liquor store."

Bobby Reese started that afternoon like any other, by walking straight to the one liquor store in the Mission that would still give him credit, Star Liquors at 22nd and South Van Ness. Hustling was tough, but it was even tougher without a breakfast beer. After convincing cashier Hassan that he was good for the money, Bobby got a 24oz malt liquor in a can.

"The beer, yes," Hassan said. "The cigarettes, no. That's too much, Bobby. You already owe us over thirty-five dollars."

"Did you say dollars or *dinars*? Hassan, you know I don't carry any *I-raq* money around on my person." It was tough to say no to Bobby Reese. Hassan shook out a couple of Marlboro Lights from his own pack and sent Bobby on his way.

Bobby cracked the beer and stuck one cigarette behind his ear, the other in his mouth, and began to walk toward 23rd Street. At two-twenty in the afternoon the sun was still high and the Mission was as warm as it ever gets. Bobby stopped to take off his jacket. He set down the beer on the sidewalk, hung the jacket on a parking meter, and was searching his pants pockets for a book of matches he was sure he had. Nothing. Typical Bobby. The gods bestow a beer and a smoke upon him and he forgets to ask for fire. He looked back at Hassan's and cursed himself for forgetting to get a light. *Pop.* There went the first shot. Bobby looked toward the corner. *Pop pop pop.* 1-2-3 more. Now Bobby did something most people don't do, Bobby ran towards the shots. He turned the corner at 23rd, looking, scanning, he saw nothing. No one. He saw the people at the ATM up on Mission Street, yeah, but no one on the corner of 23rd and Capp. *Pop.* One more.

Then Bobby knows there's trouble. He's got it triangulated. He knows where the hot spot is. He freezes up, becomes part of the scenery. Act like a tree. Be invisible. He'd been doing it his whole life. Then he saw the kid—yes, kid—running straight at him, and fuck yeah, he did look like the grim reaper. Hood up, mouth tight, gun still clenched in his hand. Running straight ahead, determined, like a linebacker.

"So you saw his face?" asked Schmitz.

"Yeah, straight at me."

"And?"

"And it looked like every other motherfucking face you see every goddamn where. Two eyes, one nose. No mustache, no beard. One fucking angry face. I'm serious, man, that fucker scared the shit outta me"

"He looked angry?"

"He looked serious."

"Was the gun in his right or left hand?"

"C'mon, man. I already done told you guys three times. It was in his right hand."

"In your initial interview with my partner, you never mentioned the Giants shirt."

"I also never said Latino." Bobby smiled.

"Come on, Bobby, why not? What else didn't you mention?"

"I was focused on the face, man, the demon. That's what was coming at me, a demon."

• • •

Ria Flores pushed open her front door with two bags of groceries.

"Oscar, Ramon? Hello? Anybody home?"

Oscar was relieved to hear his mother's voice. He hurried to the top of the stairs and rushed down to grab a bag from his mother. He felt safe now that she was home. He set down his bag on the counter and began to unpack it.

"No, no, no, Oscar, let me do it. You don't know where stuff goes."

He knew where stuff goes. He sat down at the kitchen table and watched her move from cupboard to cupboard. She looked exhausted. She made a little groan every time she put something away. It was nearly ten o'clock and she was just getting home. Oscar looked at his mother and for the first time noticed the jowly flesh gathered at the bottom of her cheeks. He noticed, too, the crow's feet reaching across her temples. His mother seemed to be aging right in front of him. Wilting.

"How was your game, sweetie?" she asked when she noticed him watching her. He loved it when she called it his game, like he was part of the team. She didn't follow baseball but she was always interested for him.

"Good, we won. 5-2. We're in second place in our division now."

"Good, honey, good. Do me a favor and put this sugar up on that top shelf, please."

Oscar got up, proud that he could be called on by his mother to perform any favor. She'd been telling him that he was a big boy since he was in training pants. Now he was starting to feel like it. He could finally be of use.

"You're getting so tall," she said, rubbing the small of his back. It was what she always did, to reassure him, to relax him, to put him to sleep. It was their own special communication.

"Have you seen your brother today?"

The spell was broken.

"I think he's in his room, sleeping."

Oscar put the bag of sugar on the counter. He looked at his mother. He waited for her to see him. She hadn't even noticed the shift, the darkening of his mood. She was already handing him a bottle of vegetable oil to go back up to the top shelf.

"Push it back now. Make sure there's enough room for the sugar to fit."

He wanted to tell her. He wanted her to stop what she was doing and listen to him. He wanted to tell her what a sick, sadistic son-of-a-bitch Ramon was. He wanted to tell the truth, he wanted her to believe him.

"Mom?"

She didn't answer, she kept right on moving.

"Mom?"

"Yes, sweetie?"

"I don't wanna live here anymore." It was all he could say; the truth was too much.

"I know, honey, we all want to move. This place is too small. There's no room to breath in here."

"No, I mean I don't want to live with Ramon anymore. I hate him."

"Oh, sweetie, he's your brother. You love each other. You're brothers." This is what she always said. She couldn't know Ramon, what he was. And she couldn't know Oscar either, not if she thought they were brothers. He was sorry he brought it up.

"Brothers don't always get along, but you're still brothers."

"I hate him."

"He's your brother."

He let it slide. There was no point in taking it any further. She finished putting the groceries away and sat down across from Oscar.

"Mom, what's for dinner?"

"Oh, sweetie, I'm too tired to make anything. I didn't even leave the salon till after nine. Just make yourself something, but clean up after yourself, okay? I'm going to bed. G'nite, I love you."

Ria got up and kissed him on the forehead. She hadn't even sat down for one whole minute. She was up and moving again, flicking off lights, picking up a few scraps of junk mail. She moved into her bedroom to continue her nightly rituals.

Oscar was left alone in the kitchen. He sat at the table pondering his options. The house grew quiet when his mother shut her bedroom door. Maybe a bowl of cereal, maybe a frozen dinner.

It was quiet but he could tell Ramon was still awake. He felt it.

Oscar decided he wasn't hungry, not hungry enough to chance disturbing his brother. He walked as lightly as he could toward his bedroom. His brother's door glared at him. The door itself was an ugly face watching Oscar slip into his room.

It took just over an hour.

Oscar was already asleep. He slept with his clothes on—like that would make a difference. The bedroom door opened. Ramon entered the room and stood there letting his eyes adjust, listening himself breathe. Oscar sensed it deep in his dreams and woke up.

Too late.

"Hold still, you piece of shit."

• • •

Alvarez lay in bed with his hands cupped behind his head. Sue lay silent beside him. He knew she wasn't asleep because he couldn't hear her light feminine snore. She was only feigning sleep. That was fine; he was tired of talking about it. Even though Vince was getting paid-leave, he'd already spent more time at the station than any day on the job he could think of. He certainly wasn't getting laid either. He worked hard to keep her happy and now that delicate balance had been thrown out of whack. Sue was becoming icy, resentful that her routine had been fucked up, fearful that her comfort zone had been disrupted. He tried to remember a positive comment, a show of sympathy, a kind word, anything she'd said about Hugh. He couldn't think of one.

In the dark he tried to go over the answers he'd given earlier that day. He wanted to form a picture in his mind, letting it develop like an old Polaroid, trying to see the figure that the whole city saw, the demon. The trick was to imagine him, but not too much. If the image became crisp and in-focus, then Vince would most definitely be cornered into a lie. But if he kept the killer's image misty, blurred, moving through reality on the corner like a dream, then Vince would only be helping by adding to the picture, providing a canvas so others could paint in the details. He tried to see him, the man he never saw.

Oscar Flores had a dream that night, or at least a vision. He saw the man across the street again, the man with the Giants T-shirt, leaning over all that blood. Only this time the man stopped what he was doing, stood straight up, turned and looked up at Oscar's window, right at him. There was a connection this time, between the man and Oscar. This time Oscar didn't see the demon that the rest of the city saw, this time Oscar saw an angel. There was an aura around him, a glow, as though an idea had flashed in the killer's mind and the man's whole body lit up like a light bulb. The killer peered up at him with one of those soft benevolent looks that reminded Oscar of the Saints frozen in stained glass inside the Mission Dolores. The killer was giving Oscar a gift.

• • •

The **SF Examiner's headline** read *Hunt for the Killer*. The *San Francisco Chronicle's* said *Eyewitness to Cop Killing*. There were some vague details about Bobby Reese's story repeated in both papers. Each piece ended with a recap of yesterday's articles and a sketch of the shooter. Neither noted that, although they now had an eyewitness, the sketch remained the same. Anonymous. Unusable. Both articles stressed that police were still looking for anyone with any kind of information. Phone numbers of homicide detectives, including Terry Schmitz's, were also listed along with the tip hotline.

On AM radio, morning talk show host Ron Owens called the killer a coward. But not as big of a coward, he said, as those eyewitnesses who hadn't yet come forward. Callers grappled with motives for the crime. Corruption and incompetence were quickly swept aside. Hugh Patterson was a victim, the ultimate victim. "He made us all victims," one caller said. "It was a hate crime of the worst kind, the hate was for us all, for society." It was a crime against the City of San Francisco.

The force and viciousness of the crime was unifying. The city emotionally banded together in their lust for vengeance. The frustrating lack of new details in the story only made their lust grow. The citizens filled in the blanks and drew their own conclusions about the killer and what should be done with him. Columnist Mitch Tatum reminded his readers about the lynch mobs of the Barbary Coast. His column was encouraging, not cautionary.

The local media's only distraction that day was the third and final game in the Giants/Dodgers series. The series was tied, one game a piece. The weather was perfect for baseball.

Oscar got up early that day, the heat from the morning sun waking him up. He sat up in bed and thought about the vision he had last night. The idea. He rejected the logic, physically shaking his body like a wet dog to rid himself of the thought. He hoped maybe the idea actually *was* a dream, one that would dissipate the further into consciousness he rose. It didn't work. The idea was still there.

He swung his legs over the side of the bed and began to dress. He thought about the game today and wondered if this afternoon would be a good time to go down to the ballpark. During several day-games last summer, Oscar would bus down to the ballpark. He would stroll amidst the throngs of fans and work his way to the back of the park. There, with their backs to McCovey Cove, fans would wait for the standing-room-only gates to swing open every third inning for a chance to watch the game for free. Oscar, waiting patiently, would slip in and see if he could peek through the elbows and hips of the standing-room-only crowd to catch a glimpse of the game. He'd been there before and felt the excitement when Pablo Sandoval hit a home run right over their heads and into the bay. He heard the cheer and looked up just in time to see the ball arcing overhead and then land with a splash behind him. People cheered, high-fived, and slapped him on the back as though he had something to do with it. Oscar felt great and he was glad he was a part of the moment. About a week later, Oscar attended when the Cleveland Indians lost after stretching it to twelve torturous innings. The damp wind whipped across the bay and seemed to funnel right into the cove as the game pushed into the night. Cold didn't seem to matter, though and the warmth of camaraderie gave off a mellow buzz. The fans stood patiently getting their money's worth watching those tense innings for free. And to pull off the win, after all that, having invested their time and hearts, all of them together, clenched against the cold. Oscar was glad he was there then, too.

Oscar pulled on his pants and listened. No sound. He stood up. No one was there.

Maybe.

If someone was there, they were asleep.

Maybe.

He eased his door open and walked lightly through the kitchen. The stillness of it made him feel guilty. He only grabbed an apple off the counter because he knew the cupboard door squeaked. The clock on the micro-wave oven read 10:10 am. He tiptoed down the stairs, careful to step on the outside of each stair. As soon as he pulled open the door he felt the cool air rush in to greet him and he stepped outside into the reassuring midday sounds of the city.

Before he walked toward the 14 Mission bus, he decided he would look at the corner. Just look. He stood there, on his side of the street, and tried to see it all over again. It was easy. All that blood. The light was different now, but Oscar could play back the scene like a movie. He could see it superimposed over the sidewalk before him. The man with the hoodie, lean-ing over. All that blood flowing down the gutter. The cop sprawled out.

All that blood.

Oscar squeezed his eyes shut and tried to push out the image of the blood. He tried to imagine only the man in the hoodie. He saw him, like a ghost right here in midday, leaning over the body. He saw him, just like the other day, but Oscar was closer now, on the side-walk, seeing it from a new vantage point. It was like an instant replay. Only this time, the man turned his head before he ran. Oscar saw it perfectly. He turned his head and looked across the street, right up at Oscar's room. Just like it happened in Oscar's dream.

Oscar snuck onto the bus through the rear door so he didn't have to pay, slipping in between the exiting bodies and finding an inconspicuous seat toward the back. He plunked himself down and was immediately met by Hugh Patterson's face. The man across from him was reading the newspaper and the picture stared down at Oscar from the front page of the *Chronicle*. Oscar looked around. There were several people reading the newspaper, all of them with the front page held high up in front of them. It was the same picture that was up on the scoreboard at the ballpark yesterday. Oscar turned away. He was getting tired of seeing the dead man's face. Then he saw the T-shirt. There was a middle-aged white woman with a 49ers hat on; she was tucked back in the corner of the bus. Her purse strap was adorned with dozens of sporting pins, mostly red and gold, some black and orange, and across her chest was the same picture that seemed to be following Oscar everywhere. There were birth and death dates stenciled on the shirt below Hugh's face along with the obligatory Rest in Peace written in calligraphy. It looked like one of those cheap iron-on tees that you can buy at the mall. Oscar wondered if the lady had it made there or if she bought it from some street vendor on Mission Street who was smart enough to be selling them.

GAME THREE

THE 14 MISSION made its way toward downtown, stopping almost every block to let people on and off. Mostly on. By the time it reached 5th Street, the bus was so full the driver refused to let anymore passengers on. After three more stops, Oscar exited the bus with a wave of others decked out in orange and black, and started the trek up 2nd Street toward AT&T Park. Most of them had loose, relaxed smiles on their faces. They had made this pilgrimage dozens of times. Although it was hours before the first pitch, there were plenty of fans milling about hoping to get there early enough to catch a glimpse of their heroes during batting practice.

Oscar looked with envy at the ticket holders lining up at the 2nd and King entrance. Small families with coolers full of drinks and snacks. Everything they could want to stuff their faces with while they watched the game. During the Indians game, a fan caught up in the moment handed Oscar a can of smuggled beer. The man smiled at Oscar as though the beer had been an invitation to a secret fraternity. The 16-oz. Miller was warm and seemed to curdle on Oscar's tongue. He would have much rather had a soda, but he drank it anyway.

As Oscar made his way around the back of the park to McCovey Cove, he noticed two more of the Hugh Patterson shirts. To Oscar, the cop and the Giants were linked. Hugh's distorted image on the T-shirts looked even more like an old baseball card, Oscar thought. Even the ginger glow of Patterson's hair and sparse freckles seemed connected to the Giants team colors.

The back of the park was not yet crowded. A few lazy kayakers paddled into the cove hoping to get souvenir homers hit out of the park. People filed off the ferries arriving for the game. A few of the ballpark regulars blended with tourists and newcomers, all jockeying to be let into the free standing-room-only section. The orange and black buckets were out again, too, taking donations. There was a slow and steady build to the crowd that turned from congestion into excitement. They gathered at the park for what they loved. Baseball.

But as Oscar stood interloping among his people, he heard the talk turn from baseball to the killing.

What should be done with the sick son-of-a-bitch, asshole, *puta* that did it, and what a good dude, guy, fellow, bro, Officer Hugh was. Did you hear he was a big Giants fan? He coached junior Giants, played Little League, beat the whole department in online fantasy baseball. He was too hard on the gangs, others said. He poked his nose in and got it shot off. He hated the drugs that consumed his neighborhood. It was an execution, he was targeted, the execution was a case of mistaken identity. A gang war that was the culprit, or a transient, a roving cop killer, a terrorist agitator dressed up to look like a gangbanger. The crowd was distracted, obsessed. They were ignoring the real reason they'd assembled. Oscar cocked his head left and right, letting the comments ricochet around him. He wished that they'd go back to talking about baseball.

It wasn't until the fifth inning, when they displayed the picture of Hugh Patterson again, that Oscar thought about it. There was no avoiding it. It had been at him all day, staring him in the face. He had to think about it, his dream. That asshole, that creep, that *puta*, that motherfucker looking right up at him. Practically smiling.

The people around him hushed as the loudspeaker crackled something about Hugh. Oscar couldn't make out what it was; he just watched the intent faces around him. Then a cheer went up and the people around him clapped and nodded approvingly.

"Fifty thousand," someone said.

"Don't matter if it's a hundred," said someone else.

And Oscar looked up, craning his neck to see the scoreboard from the free section, and saw Hugh's face, impossibly huge, stretched, distorted, and glowing. It was a sixty-foot aura. He could feel the reverent buzz in the crowd as they all gazed up silently at the image. Hugh's face hung there above them: electric, begging for justice, begging for some sense to be made out of his life. Practically smiling.

• • •

Detective Terry Schmitz was sitting at his desk, not sure if the uncomfortable feeling in his stomach was hunger or indigestion. He eyed his coffee cup with suspicion. He really ought to give that shit up. He felt a gurgle. Caffeine was one of his only vices left and he didn't like how the stuff dictated his days.

The phone on his desk rang. He answered the call and instinctively picked up his coffee mug and took a sip. It was the first call today. Yesterday it had been crank callers, well wishers, and even a deluded confession. Not one usable tip.

"Detective Schmitz."

"I saw the guy," was all the voice said. He couldn't tell for sure, but Schmitz thought the voice belonged to a boy.

"What guy?"

"The guy you're looking for."

"And where did you see him?" Terry had already taken tips from concerned citizens that saw the killer on a bus, drinking wine out of a bag at 6th and Market Street, driving a taxi cab, and one caller claimed that the murderer was bussing tables at Zuni's. Not since the Zodiac Killings had there been so many sightings of a suspect. The vague everyman quality of the sketch wasn't helping. All these tips were supposed to be followed up on, but Terry had already decided to only go for the ones that set off an alarm, his intuition. The kind of feeling that rose up inside of him when he heard the boy's voice.

"Where?" said the voice, sounding confused.

"Where did you think you saw the perpetrator?"

"On the corner. I saw him do it."

Terry froze. Eyewitness. He carefully set down his coffee cup, as though a spill might frighten the caller away. He looked at his phone and scribbled down the number on the caller ID.

"I'm gonna need some more information, Mr. …?"

"Flores. Oscar Flores. I live at 799 Capp. Right at 23rd."

"Well, Oscar, when might be a good time when we could talk further?" Terry was talking slow, drawing out his words while he frantically searched through his yellow legal pad for the kid's name. "If you like, we can come over and talk right now."

"No. Maybe I should come see you."

"It's no problem. We can come to you, give you a ride down here. Whatever you think."

"No, I'll come see you. I'll come today, this afternoon. I promise." And the boy hung up. Terry sat with the receiver still pressed against his ear. Then, with his freshly sharpened pencil, he circled a tiny note he'd made two days ago at the bottom of his yellow pad. It said, *Ria Flores, 45, son Ramon 20, 799 Capp, upstairs.* Below it was written, *inside, nothing.*

Oscar felt sick when he hung up the phone. He didn't know if he could go through with his plan. After the game he'd bussed home and walked two blocks to the 24th Street BART station where there were pay-phones tucked on the mezzanine level, above the trains but below the street. He stood there, staring straight ahead, feeling clammy and cold; commuters walking right by, stepping around him. He was invisible. Like a ghost—no, like a thief.

A derelict sat nearby, piled like trash on top of a near crushed cardboard box. It looked like he had been in the same spot for months. There was a dirty top hat at his feet turned upside down for charity of any kind. He was bloated, diseased looking. Greasy dirt marks creased his face. Underneath the filth, Oscar saw something familiar. The bum wore that same smile, that same damn smile that was on the kill-er's face, and on Hugh's. The bum kept looking right at him, like he knew something. Smiling with his eyes now, not breaking his stare. What did he know? Oscar frowned, tried to give him his hard look, and started for the escalator.

• • •

"Yes, they want me back in today. It's fucking relentless. That a-hole Schmitz has done a 180 on me, completely turned. Fucking asshole thinks I shot my own partner, I swear."

Sue watched her husband pace back and forth across the room clutching his phone. The pacing wasn't enough to feed his agitation; he knocked on counters, straightened pictures, opened and closed the refrigerator door.

"Look, fuck this. You guys need to dip into the fund and get me a real lawyer. What do you mean, what do I have to worry about? A fucking miscarriage of justice, that's what."

Sue could tell that the sound had stopped on the other end of the phone. Vince had stopped talking, too. She squinted at him, tried to read his thoughts, gauge the look in his eyes, but he wouldn't stand still long enough. The conversation started again.

"No, my story has not changed, not one bit. I think he's just got a hard-on 'cause he has no leads, not real ones. I don't know what the fuck he wants with me.

I don't know what it is he wants to hear me say. It's a fucking agenda. I don't know what to tell you."

She watched him cross over to the kitchen counter and light a cigarette. He hadn't smoked in years, not since he went into the academy, and there he was, smoking, inside the apartment, with no ashtray and no window open. She didn't understand. She didn't understand why this was happening. Vince didn't commit the crime, and he wasn't the one who got shot. He lost his partner; it could have been him dead in the street. Why were they focused on Vince? Why did his testimony matter so much? He wasn't there, he couldn't have helped. Sue sat with her hand over her mouth, desperately wanting to ask questions.

● ● ●

Piss hitting the urinal porcelain always sounded metallic to Schmitz. It reminded him of the god awful metal shitters they have in the holding cells. He hated that the john was the cop equivalent of the water cooler, the only place where they felt vulnerable enough to let their guard down, a level playing field where things were off the record. Terry didn't like being talked to when he was doing his business. Didn't matter if it was about a case or last night's game, it could wait till he got to the fucking sink.

"What's up with Patterson?"

He knew it. Couldn't even take a piss without

somebody bringing up this case. You couldn't tell someone to fuck off. It was a cop-killer case, everybody was concerned. You couldn't tell them you had nothing; that'd be worse. You couldn't shrug your shoulders because then you'd piss on your shoe.

"Not much. New eyewitness, I hope." He kept his head straight down when he spoke. Christ, he didn't want to make eye contact with someone while he was taking a piss.

"Who, that crack-head? I already heard about him."

"Actually he's not a crack-head, he may be a bit of a drinker. But, no, someone else—a kid." Schmitz turned toward the sinks to wash his hands and watched the other cop move straight toward the door. Obnoxious *and* unhygienic, nice.

"No shit, a wino and a tyke. Good luck with that, Schmitz."

Terry felt pressure at his neck. He could feel his pulse beat against the stiff collar of his shirt. He immediately regretted giving up any information. Assholes, he murmured under his breath, and continued washing his hands. This was no toddler. There was something about this kid, something that made Schmitz believe him.

He'd had Oscar Flores picked up while he waited on Mission Street for his bus. They didn't want him getting lost—or scared—on the way down to the Hall of Justice. Terry watched the patrolmen bring him in through the office. The kid was shook to the core, Schmitz sensed it. Presently they had him stored up in interview room number six. Schmitz was only waiting for the tech guy to set up the recording equipment.

Oscar sat quietly with his hands folded in front of him. The room reminded Oscar of school. The tables, the carpet, the walls. Everything but the two cameras mounted high above him in the corners of the room. His listened to the air blowing through the ventilator. It gave off a pulsating whir. He listened hard for any other sound and there was none. None he could hear, just the loud unsteady whir of the air.

He finally heard a throat clearing. An announcement. The door opened and in came a man Oscar thought could have easily passed for a science teacher at his junior high. The man smiled, introduced himself, and sat down.

"Oscar, I'm Detective Schmitz. You can call me Terry."

Oscar didn't say a word.

"Okay then, let's get started. This is all going to be recorded, all right? First, I'm gonna say our names and what time it is and where we are. Then, I'm gonna ask you some questions, okay?"

Oscar still didn't respond. He was waiting for the interview to begin. The detective didn't speak into a microphone. He stated the necessary information to no one in particular, speaking to the open air of the room. Oscar glanced up and saw both cameras had tiny glowing red lights. After the preliminary statements, Schmitz flipped open his yellow legal pad, wet the tip of his pencil on his tongue, and began, "Okay Oscar, let's start with where you were when you heard the shots."

"I was in my room."

"In your room at 799 Capp Street?"

"Yes."

Terry stopped to write something down.

"What were you doing?"

"Looking out the window."

"Before that, what were you doing before the shots?"

Oscar paused. This was it. This was the point of no return.

"Watching the game."

Terry saw his opening. "You a baseball fan, Oscar?" He saw Oscar blink. It wasn't quite a smile, but it was enough. "Hell of a series. Fucking Dodgers, eh?"

"Yeah," Oscar agreed. The Dodgers comment caught him off-guard. It reminded Oscar of the being at the ballpark, the innocent but gruff exchanges with like-minded strangers. The ice was broken.

"You remember when?" Terry asked.

Oscar thought maybe it was an unfinished question about baseball. He raised his eyebrows and waited for the detective to complete the question.

"The window, do you remember when you got up to look out of the window?"

Oscar paused so it would seem like he was thinking about the question, but he knew exactly when. "Top of the sixth."

Terry wrote this down.

"So why did you get up? I mean, it's not the seventh-inning stretch. Why take your eyes off the game?"

"I was nervous for them, the team. I always do it when it gets too tense. I pace. I can sit still when we're winning."

"Or losing." Terry's statement meant that they were moving on.

"What did you see when you looked out the window?"

"I saw it."

"You saw what, Oscar?"

"I saw that policeman get shot."

Terry looked at Oscar, getting a feel for the weight of that statement, authenticating it.

"Was the officer standing up or already laying down when you saw him?"

"He was standing up, I saw him get shot in the face. I saw him fall. I saw everything."

"What about the guy doing the shooting? Did you see him, too?"

Oscar nodded.

Terry needed his response on tape. "Oscar, did you see him too?"

"Yes. I saw him. I saw him lean over and shoot that man over and over."

"Did you see what the guy looked like?"

"When he was finished he turned and looked right at me, right up at my window."

"What did he look like, Oscar, can you describe him?"

There was a long silence. Once again, the only sound in the room was the air moving through the vents. Terry couldn't tell if Oscar was forming a picture in his head, reliving the events, or just scared shitless. Terry waited and tried not to seem impatient.

Finally Oscar said it.

"I know him."

Terry tried to contain his excitement. "You know him? Do you think you could recognize him again?"

"I know him," Oscar repeated. "He's my brother."

The answer flew right by Terry. He sat still, waiting for the boy to give a description. The silence went on.

"He's my brother. He looked right at me."

Terry was still. He was looking hard into the boy's eyes. He was searching for pain, the electrical impulses that resonated into the eyes, the tamped-down emotion that is so virulent that the irises seem to vibrate. Terry knew instantly there was truth in what the boy was saying. The suspect had looked right at him to check. It was instinct. The perp was looking back at his own home. Like the dope fiend who glances at his stash when cops show up, he probably couldn't help it. The killer peeked at the only place his conscience was able to shine a pinhole light, his home right across the street. And his little brother, this kid sitting right in front of Schmitz, saw the whole goddamn thing.

"Your brother is Ramon Flores?" Detective Schmitz speaking for the record again.

"Yes."

"Describe him."

Forty-five minutes later, Terry had to piss. The kid was doing fine, it was Terry who needed a break. The cold air of the men's restroom cleared his head. For once it was quiet in there. He drew a deep breath that was scented with disinfectant. He pissed. Schmitz was already washing his hands before being interrupted by another detective coming through the door.

"Hey Schmitty, I hear you got the kid in there."

"Oh yeah, I got him. The kid is the case. We're hanging on to him."

"Really? Sounds solid. What did he say?"

"Says his brother is the shooter."

"What? Get the fuck outta here. It's bullshit. Why is he coming in three days later?"

"That's exactly why he waited. His brother is a fucking psychopath. Guy still lives in the same house, which is across the street from the crime scene, by the way. No wonder the kid's a little nervous."

"Seems a little too easy, Schmitty. Give up anything else? Hand you the gun, too?"

Terry turned off the faucet and shook the water off his hands. He turned and, for the first time, looked into the eyes of the other detective.

"Anything else? Anything else? Fucking eyewitness to the crime, positive ID that matches two other witnesses, one of whom is a goddamned cop. I'd say that's pretty good. It's enough for an arrest, that's for sure."

"Well, thank God for that, Schmitty. Maybe this city can get some sleep now."

The detective disappeared into a stall. Terry hated being called Schmitty. He never let it happen when he was a kid and another cop was the only one who could get away with it now. Maybe after his inevitable promotion he'd make these assholes address him by rank only. They were colleagues, not friends. All of them, he reminded himself.

Terry Schmitz looked at himself in the mirror, knowing that soon his face would be on TV. He looked at his face, trying to imagine what people would see when seeing him for the first time. He was handsome, he thought, clean cut, chiseled. He had a look, the look of authority, the look of a problem solver. He had the look of a hero. This case was going to move this face forward.

In the interrogation room, Oscar sat looking at the mirror, too. He was wondering who was behind the two-way glass framed across the room from him. He imagined a small team of tech experts with headphones covering their ears. They were probably back there tweaking knobs and adjusting levels. He thought about them. He didn't think about Ramon. He didn't think about his mother. He looked hard at the two-way glass, trying to look through it. He could only see himself.

• • •

"C'mon, Salty, enough. Pass that thing over."

The sweet smoke of the tobacco, mixed with the fruity smell of the green bud, set off a Pavlovian response in Ramon. His mouth actually watered. He hated it when Salty lit the blunt. It took him forever to pass it.

"C'mon, greedy-ass."

Ramon and Salty sat on top of two plastic milk crates in the parking lot of a small supermarket a couple of blocks from Ramon's house. They sat sharing a blunt, each of them with a 40-oz. beer wrapped in the obligatory brown paper bag clutched in their hands. Ramon took his first hit off the long, thin, brown cigar and felt the hot smoke expand in his lungs. The familiar acrid burn was immediately comforting. He held it there for a few seconds before emitting a stream of grey-blue smoke.

"Man, Ramon, I'm telling you, I could grow this shit in my closet at home. It's easy. An extension cord for the lights. My old man would never know."

"Bullshit," Ramon said, clearing his throat, "He'd smell that shit in a heartbeat."

"Nah, man, he never goes up there, he hates seeing me in my natural habitat, drives him crazy."

"It drives him crazy 'cause he pays the rent on your habitat, dumbass."

"Whatever—," Salty interrupted himself to take another hit off the blunt. Short, quick, audible hits, like little sips, sucking right off the end of the blunt, it looked like he was kissing it. It drove Ramon crazy. No wonder Salty's old man couldn't stand him.

Salty finally passed the blunt back to Ramon, who drew deeply and held the smoke tight in his lungs.

"Don't fucking move," was the next thing he heard. There was only a second to register that it was not Salty. It was someone else's voice. Then there was a hot, white explosion of pain at the back of his skull. Someone had hit him, hard. That same someone was now tackling him forward, pushing him off the milk crate, collapsing him to the ground. He felt the bits of loose gravel and ground-up glass scrape his face while his cheek was pushed against the pavement. Blunt smoke expired out of his lungs.

The world was horizontal now. He felt someone holding his head down, pushing it hard with the palm of their hand. His limbs were being pulled out from under him. He felt many sets of hands on his body. He heard radios transmitting. The static language of police code. He saw boots. They weren't the kind of footwear that patrolmen wear. They looked like military issue, the kind the SWAT team wore. And there were a lot of them.

• • •

The **SF Examiner's headline** read *Got Him!* It quoted DA Harris promising swift justice and had the Police Chief Buchwald claiming there was never any doubt the killer would be apprehended. There was talk of the death penalty and outrage that the suspect was only twenty years old. Details were vague, but it didn't matter. The tone of the information and comments from police sources were triumphant. The case had been solved.

"What are you doing here? I thought you were gettin' paid to stay home."

The officer standing in front of Alvarez's desk was cheery enough, but Vince was startled. He'd just logged onto the interdepartmental computer and his focus was on the screen.

"I'm just here picking up some shit out of my desk."

"You hear the news?"

Everyone had heard the news. Alvarez saw the headline plastered against the front of the newspaper machines as he walked into the Hall of Justice. (He'd already heard about the boy witness. Although he wasn't at the office, he wasn't out of the gossip loop entirely.) Every cop he was friendly enough with to give a passing nod felt the need to say something to him about the arrest. The accolades rubbed him the wrong way. Vince felt as though he was being exonerated for something he never did.

"Yeah, I heard."

"You should get outta here and enjoy your time off. This investigation's gonna be over soon and you're gonna be back on the beat."

"I'll do that." Alvarez smiled as a way of ending the conversation. The well-wisher took the hint and walked away. This guy, thought Vince, telling him he should be enjoying himself right after his partner was gunned down in the street. What an asshole.

With his colleague gone, Alvarez went back to the police database—the real reason he came from the Sunset all the way down to the Hall of Justice. He tapped in the name he remembered Patterson saying. The name of the thug they'd run into that day: Miguel Martinez. The screen quickly clogged with a long list of arrest records with the name Miguel Martinez. Alvarez blew out a gust of air and started going through them, trying to shorten the list with an estimated birthdate.

It took a few minutes, but he finally clicked on the Miguel Martinez that seemed to fit the bill. A scowling mug shot filled the screen. It was him, the kid they saw on Capp Street right before the shooting. Vince scrolled down to the attached arrest record. Possession of narcotics, conspiracy to distribute methamphetamine, assault, assault with a deadly weapon, resisting arrest. The list went on. Vince wondered why this punk was still on the street, but the story was all there. The ratio of arrests and convictions was out of balance. Miguel Martinez had served mostly jail time with a short stint in prison for commercial burglary.

Vince pulled up Miguel's picture again and stared at it. The dark eyes scowled back from the monitor. Vince felt a terrible pit in his stomach. Could this be the man that murdered his partner? If so, who were they holding? Had the boy witness seen this photo? He'd told Schmitz they'd run into Martinez before the shooting, but Schmitz didn't seem interested. He seemed more concerned with why Alvarez wasn't at his partner's side. Fucking Schmitz would rather hang a fellow officer out to dry than chase down the real perp.

He grabbed a few items from his desk—stuff he didn't need, but thought would bolster his excuse for being there—and headed for the door. From the moment he'd walked in, he couldn't wait to get out of the Hall of Justice.

As he stood up from his desk, his cell rang in his pocket. Vince dug it out and looked at the ID. A 553 number. SFPD. He hit the answer button and said hello.

Schmitz's voice came over the line.

"Vince, this is Terry Schmitz. How're you doing today?"

"What do you want, Schmitz?"

"We're putting together a line-up this afternoon and I'd like you to be there. Can you make it?"

Asking was Schmitz's way of letting Vince know it was not a request, but an order.

Vince Alvarez took one last look at Miguel Martinez's face before reaching over and powering down his computer.

"I'll be there."

Ria Flores was picked up from the salon where she worked about twenty minutes before they got Ramon. Terry Schmitz had her sealed off in an interrogation room, the same room where he had interviewed Oscar. She sat crying before the two-way glass, watching her mascara run in its reflection.

Terry Schmitz sat behind the glass watching the video-feed. He saw her clearly through the two-way, but with the video he could zoom in and watch the shifting emotions on her face. He rubbed his chin thoughtfully. He did this when he didn't know what else to do. He wanted to glean something from the mother, read her for some kind of clue, but he had no idea what. She sat, bewildered, sequestered, weeping steadily for the last two hours. They were running out of stalls. It was only fear that kept her in that seat; the fear that if she stepped out of that room she'd have to face it all over again. She might have to hear that it was true, what she'd been told. Terry could see she believed, in the deepest way, that her son was innocent, that he was inside her home when the crime occurred. How could she see it any other way? Terry watched, listened to her sobs, and rubbed his chin.

What Ria Flores didn't know was that both her sons were being held in that building. The identities of both witnesses, Oscar and Bobby Reese, were withheld from the media. Ria had no idea where Oscar was; she hadn't seen him since last night. But she knew right where Ramon was. Terry watched her quiver in the monitor and wondered if it meant something.

Terry had spent the last hour talking to reporters, giving guarded information and trying not to get tripped up by any questions. Playing department spokesperson wasn't as easy as it looked, but he could get used to it. They'd try the old one-two: toss you a softball, and then hit you with another question before you took a breath. Suddenly you were answering when you should be keeping your mouth shut. They'd been at their jobs longer than he'd been playing media star, but he knew he was smarter. He could handle the press. They were, after all, only citizens.

The sparring drained him though, and he sought refuge in the tech room. He sat alone in there, waiting. He was waiting for the other two witnesses to be brought in to ID Ramon. He was waiting for the door to open and the bright office light to spill in and give him an instant headache. Soon, someone would pull him out for some task that they could easily figure out on their own. He wanted just a few more minutes in the dark, listening, trying to decode the long and steady rhythm of Ria Flores' sobs.

• • •

"You know the drill, bud."

Bud. It pissed Alvarez off. He hated being called *bud*. It was almost as bad as being called *guy*. Vince stood behind the glass beside Terry Schmitz, DA Harris, and two of the DA's henchmen. One shy tech sat behind them with his headphones on. The room was dim and silent. On the other side of the glass the platform was empty. They all looked blankly at the blue horizontal stripes indicating height. 4', 5', 6'. Their anticipation made the platform seem like a stage.

"Tell 'em we're ready," Terry said to the tech.

A door opened and an antiseptic white light filled the platform. Six young men walked slowly up onto the platform. They stood there, facing straight ahead, waiting for instructions.

"Turn toward the window," the tech said into the mike.

The six men turned together and Alvarez saw that they all wore Giants shirts. The same design, the one with the word Giants splayed across a baseball. The logo seemed familiar and friendly to Vince. Out of place.

"What do you think?" Terry asked. "You want me to have 'em turn around? Say anything?"

"I dunno."

But Alvarez did know. He looked at those six faces, each of them barely distinguishable from the next. He wanted this to be over more than anything. He missed his partner, but he wanted his life back. He looked at those six faces, trying to take his time.

He knew who Ramon Flores was; it was his beat. He'd seen him and his brother around the neighborhood. It was his job. Maybe reporters couldn't find out who the boy-wonder was, but cops loved to gossip. Word was all over the Mission Station about who the young witness was. Vince got three phone calls before Schmitz even called him in for the line-up. Vince Alvarez knew exactly who Ramon Flores was.

He looks just like him, thought Vince. He looks just like the guy Bobby Reese described. Shit, they all did, but Ramon really fit the bill. Vince looked hard at him.

An assessment. A judgment. Could this kid have done it? Could that really be the cold-hearted piece of shit that shot my partner? His gut was talking, but he only listened to his head.

"Well, what do you think?" Terry asked again.

"Number four."

"Number four, step forward," repeated the tech.

Ramon stepped forward. There was fear in his eyes. Nothing else. No sign of any deep buried guilt. He didn't know why he was there, had no idea what possible piece of evidence could drag him into such a nightmare. He only felt fear. Cold, tactile, instinctual fear.

Terry held his breath and waited for Alvarez to make his decision. The boy had been easy, going through the motions, identifying his own brother. *Strike one.* Bobby Reese took a little longer, but not much. Bobby thought for a minute that it could have been number two. But then Bobby smartened up and came around and picked Ramon. *Strike two.* Now it was up to Alvarez, the cop. Irreproachable evidence. Identification by one of San Francisco's finest would be the last nail he needed.

Vince decided. It was enough. He wanted this to be over more than anyone.

"Number four."

"Are you sure?"

"I'm sure."

Terry rubbed his hands together and turned toward DA Harris. He tried not to grin. "You heard him."

DA Harris pursed her lips together and nodded.

Terry let it out, a thin shallow smile.

Strike three.

EXTRA INNINGS

OSCAR WAS A HERO. The city had their killer. Three eyewitnesses. Three strikes. Oscar couldn't explain why it fell into place like that. He could only guess that things were the way they were supposed to be. It was God working in his life. Hard to believe, though. Why would God look out for Oscar? He'd never been there to save him before. Even when Ramon was on him and he prayed for God's help. Maybe it was Hugh Patterson, stepping in from the heavens for one last good deed.

Oscar's identity was kept a secret. He overheard people in the Mission talking about the boy-witness in exalted terms. The accolades made him feel good, a part of something bigger. But back on his block, where people knew both him and Ramon, the feeling was not so pleasant. Oscar's face seemed to bring up a subject the neighborhood wanted to forget. He was a living reminder of the crime, an unavoidable connection by blood. The community would never be able to sever him from his brother's guilt. There was judgment, confusion, and very little empathy. How could they understand? Oscar told himself, they didn't know.

Days turned to weeks and Oscar watched the baseball season crawl by. The Giants leapfrogged all over the National League West. Oscar tried to stay focused on the team, but baseball was slowly eclipsed by the upcoming trial. The summer had thrust him forward toward adulthood long before he was ready.

Their home was quiet now that his brother was gone. The dark door to Ramon's room remained closed and Oscar did his best not to look at it. He moved about the apartment normally now, like he lived there, like he belonged. And at night, he slept the deep sleep that children sleep. When he woke in the morning, his mother had usually gone to work. It was just Oscar and his thoughts, alone in the house. He felt calm, independent, grown-up. Oscar liked the feeling. He felt no guilt.

Oscar sat at the kitchen table, the sports page spread out before him. A portable TV on the kitchen counter blasted cartoons that Oscar ignored. He spooned heaping wet lumps of cereal into his mouth, not worrying about the milk dribbling down his chin. This is how Oscar forgot about Ramon, by losing himself in the simple pleasures of being fifteen.

"Hello, Oscar? You here?"

Ria had arrived home early. The salon's manager had been sympathetic to Ria ever since the story broke. She'd have sent Ria home everyday if she didn't believe her work at the salon was helping hold the poor woman together. At some point, though, the tears became too much, bad for business, and she had to ask Ria to head out early.

Oscar heard the door shut, the familiar creak of the footsteps, and waited for his mother to appear at the top of the stairs. He didn't wipe his chin or reach for the volume on the TV.

Ria appeared at the top of the stairs looking completely disconnected from the bright voice Oscar had heard moments before. The woman at the top of the stairs looked tired, beaten. Oscar knew that what he'd done had aged his mother. He clung to the hope that the reward money would change all that. He would buy his mother makeovers, days at the spa. She would go to the big salons and sit as a customer instead of sweeping up the hair clippings of those that could afford it. He thought of that reward money as the greatest Christmas gift he could ever give his mother and he guarded the hope like a secret surprise.

"Oscar, sweetie, we need to talk."

He could tell by her eyes that she'd been crying

again. Puffy and red and ringed with darkness. They'd been through this before. She'd ask him why, and he'd say that she wouldn't understand. Then the tears would really flow. Oscar would squeeze her hand. His mother would squeeze back, hard. He would feel her fingernails biting into his palm.

If they could just get through this pain, clamp their eyes together so tight that they could squeeze the pain out, then they would be okay, be normal, like everyone else.

"Make me understand."

"Mama ..." He already heard sobs choking in the back of her throat.

"Just tell me why. Why you did this. How did this happen? Why wasn't he upstairs? I thought he was upstairs. I *know* he was upstairs."

"Mama, we've been through this. He wasn't upstairs. He wasn't who you think he was, I promise. I didn't do anything—you didn't do anything. It's not our fault— none of it."

It was hard for Oscar to watch the confusion in his mother's eyes as they darted back and forth searching him for some new information. She wanted answers, but she only wanted the answers she wanted to hear.

He wanted to tell her. He wanted to tell the whole truth. About why Ramon faltered when they pressed him for what he was doing the moment the shots were fired. Ramon looked scared and guilty because he was.

About why he hated Ramon and why Ramon's crimes were just as bad as murder.

"If he was upstairs, then how could this thing happen? Why did you say this thing happened?"

Here it came.

"Why didn't you say he was upstairs?"

Oscar looked right at her. She was lost. The tears in her eyes welled up and spilled down her cheeks. His mother thought this thing could be undone. Maybe Oscar would apologize, think maybe it wasn't Ramon. What was the word? *Recant.* She believed her son was innocent. It made no sense to her. Ramon was not capable of this kind of destruction.

Oscar knew otherwise. Oscar knew Ramon was a sadistic son-of-a-bitch. His mother, though, would never accept that such a sick, twisted pervert had sprung from her loins, was somehow a part of her. Oscar wanted to tell his mother that what he did made it right. He had found a way to make sense out of it. It was a gift. He used the gift to make things right. Ramon ended up where he belonged and, now, he and his mother were going to be able to have a life.

Oscar sat, lips pinched tight. They'd been over this ground again and again for the last several weeks. There was nothing he was going to say that she wanted to hear.

"Mama …" was all he could say. He let it hang there. It was left open-ended, like a promise, ambiguous and unfulfilled. He couldn't say another word. He wanted to. Maybe after the reward. Reminding himself about the reward strengthened him. It gave him stamina for her pain. He pushed the cereal bowl aside and reached across the table to offer his hand. She took it and squeezed.

That night Oscar dreamed he was pitching for the Giants. He stood on the mound far away from home plate. The crowd was there. He could feel them. He couldn't see any of them—not one—but he could feel them. They were expecting a pitch. Home plate seemed impossibly far away. He'd never thrown a ball that kind of distance before. He looked up at the scoreboard and saw Ramon's junior year school photo stretched across the screen. Oscar looked away. The catcher was signaling but he was too far away. Oscar couldn't make out the catcher's hand signs. He stood there, trying to look like he was winding up. He kept the ball tucked away in his glove and waited, terrified.

Finally the catcher began the long walk out to the mound. Oscar waited for him. He noticed for the first time the light and heat of the midday sun. The closer the catcher got, the more Oscar became aware of his uniform. It was real Giants gear. It was an affirmation of the dream. It was really happening. He saw the thick official seams disappearing beneath the professional leather catcher pads. He heard the creak of the equipment as the player stepped up onto the mound. The catcher looked right at Oscar and lifted his mask. It was Hugh Patterson, smiling the same smile from the photograph. He looked happy and relaxed, like baseball itself. The pressure wasn't bothering him at all.

"Kid, just throw the ball. Everything'll be fine. Just throw that thing right over the plate."

• • •

It was about two months after the trial. Vince Alvarez was back on duty with his new partner, David Cho. Cho was about as tired of hearing about Patterson as Alvarez was, so he never brought up the subject. And that was just fine by Vince Alvarez. The sooner the city got back to business-as-usual the better.

About two hours into their shift, they got a call about an adolescent shoplifter at a liquor store at 22nd and Bryant. By the time Vince and his partner got there, the kid had bolted from the shop. Officer Cho waited by the door while Vince talked to the owner.

"You need to do something about this," the shop owner said from behind the counter.

"Now, sir, I understand it can be frustrating—"

"These kids, they come and steal from me every day—*every day*—and no one does anything about it. They're criminals—all if them. They'll all end up dead or in jail. Where are their parents? You need to do something."

"Me?" Vince said, trying not to sound as annoyed as he was.

"Yes, you," the man behind the counter said. "You wear a uniform, but you're not the police. You work for the government, but you are not the police. Police help people. You don't help. If you don't arrest these boys today, tomorrow they will be back with guns and knives."

Vince wanted to say something, but he faltered. He wanted to explain to the man about priorities, about procedure, about taking personal responsibility, but it was bullshit. Vince knew it and the liquor store owner would too. Vince shrugged his shoulders at the shop owner and walked back to the patrol car, flanked by his partner.

Climbing into the driver's seat, Alvarez saw four young men leaning on a wall across the street, three of them with 40-oz. bottles of beer partially obscured by their legs in an attempt at discretion. Vince sat in the car and looked at them from behind his pilot's glasses. The young men knew they were being watched and pantomimed casual talk. As the minutes ticked by, they grew more relaxed, forgetting about the patrol car perched across the street.

Vince recognized Miguel Martinez right away. He wore the same smirk that he wore on the day of the murder. Vince felt a warm burn right in the middle of his chest. The pain sharpened. He couldn't tell if it was his stomach or his heart. His partner climbed into the passenger seat and spun the car's laptop around.

"Everything all right?" he asked Alvarez.

"Sure, let's get rolling," said Vince, but they both sat there.

Vince's new partner waited for him to start the car. Vince just sat with his hands on the wheel, watching the young men across the street. That was Martinez all right. He'd recognize him anywhere. He looked exactly the same as he did that day on Capp Street. Except for one thing. It would have made Alvarez smile if the pain in his chest wasn't already making him wince. Miguel Martinez was wearing a brand new Dodgers shirt.

His lucky shirt.

POSTGAME

They'd only gone a few blocks when Vince pulled over again.

"What're you doing?" asked his partner.

"I thought we'd wait by a stop sign. Write up some easy ones for a change. Take a break."

"We just took lunch thirty minutes ago. We still have to go by that spot on Guerrero, we promised the priest we'd check out the vandalism at his church."

"It's not a church. It's a school."

"Whatever."

Vince parallel parked the prowl car on Alabama, giving them a perfect vantage point for the four-way stop at 23rd Street.

Officer Cho asked, "You mind if I smoke?"

Sounding tired and distracted, Vince said, "Yes, I mind. I mind every time you ask. I just fucking quit. Again. I'm not trying to start."

"What's going on with you, man?"

At first Vince didn't answer, then, after a few moments, he said, "I lied."

David Cho didn't respond. He wasn't sure where his partner was going with this.

"That day with Hugh? I lied. I left him standing in front of the taqueria. I walked away."

"You weren't there when the shots were fired. I know, I heard."

"No, it's not just that. I walked away. I should have been there. I was calling my fucking wife."

"Look, man, sometimes these things—"

"No, you don't understand. I lied. I didn't want to admit I was off somewhere on the phone when my partner was being murdered, so I stretched the truth."

The car was quiet except for the low steady crackle of the police radio. David Cho didn't say anything else. He waited for the confession to unravel.

"It got away from me. During the interviews. I acted like I was closer than I was." Vince kept his eyes forward, staring at the intersection in front of them. Not one car had gone through. "I couldn't explain why I didn't see anything. I mean, I said I was on the alley when it happened, I should have seen something. They kept asking about the timing. How many seconds and how many shots and where were you by the time you heard the first shot, the second, the third. They kept asking questions and the truth just kind of slipped away. I didn't want it to; it just did. They figured I must have seen something by the time that piece of shit stuck the gun under Hugh's chin."

"What *did* you see?"

"Nothing. That's my point. I didn't see shit. I wasn't there at all. I was checking up on my goddamn wife. I told them I maybe saw someone running away, but I didn't see shit." He gripped the steering wheel with both hands. "Until today."

"What do you mean?"

"Over there, at the liquor store, there were some kids drinking forties, over by the wall. You see 'em?"

"Yeah, I saw them."

"The one with the Dodger shirt and the greasy mustache. Me and Hugh saw him right before it happened. I'd pushed it out of my mind."

"So what?" David Cho said, but he already knew where this was going.

"He fits. The description, the time frame. Nobody looked at him after the kid came forward. The kid said his bit and everything else fell into place. I know I did."

"They *all* fit the description." As soon as Cho said it, he realized he wasn't making his partner feel any better. He tried to change the subject. "Was your wife okay?"

"Yeah," Alvarez said, "She was just fine."

Sue Alvarez finished her work out early. She usually spent close to an hour at the gym, but today she was there only twenty minutes. Every Tuesday now was a short work out. She walked in the door to their apartment and tossed her gym bag on the floor. She only had a few minutes.

First she turned her cell phone's ringer down. Not off, just down. Then she poured herself a tall glass of cranberry juice. Before she took the first sip the doorbell rang. She buzzed the front door without using the intercom. Footsteps came bounding up the apartment building's marble stairs and she opened the front door before they reached her floor.

"Yuri. What took you so long?"

"I showered real quick at the gym. I wanted to be clean for you."

"You're all clean? No fair. I have to wait till we're done to shower."

"That's all right. You're like a little bit of sweet and a little bit of salty. Just the way I like it."

He tried to grab her right there in the hall, but she stopped him. Instead she pulled him by his shirt into the apartment, saying, "Not out here. C'mon. We don't have much time."

Inside, they went through their ritual. Peeling the

clothes off one another while they kissed, trying to not break their embrace as the garments fell to the floor. When they were ready, she reached an arm around his neck and started to steer him toward the couch.

"Let's go in the bedroom," he said. "Just this once."

It killed the mood for a moment. At once, she went from playful to serious "You know we can't do that. I'm not doing laundry all afternoon." Sue's tone dried up entirely. "What would Vince think? Coming home to washed sheets? He's nosey enough as it is."

Being admonished in this maternal fashion didn't slow Yuri down. He wrapped his arm around her waist and lifted her up as he stepped backward to the couch. "The couch will be fine," he said. "Better, in fact."

• • •

"What are you trying to say?"

David Cho was watching his partner's expression, but Vince had his gaze locked onto the intersection in front of them.

"It's just … I don't know. This is the first time I've seen him, that's all. Since that day."

"And what? You're having second thoughts?"

"No," Vince said. But after another moment of motionless thought, he added, "I don't know. The kid's brother never made sense to me. This other one, the one at the liquor store, he's a fucking dark angel. Bad news. You should see this scumbag's rap sheet. We saw him that day. Right before it happened."

"Where?"

"On Capp Street. Right there. Right on the same spot."

"Jesus, Vince. You picked the kid's brother out of a lineup."

Silence filled the car once again.

"We're talking about a cop killer here," Cho said. "You're saying you're not sure now if the guy you helped finger is good for the deed? That's a pretty big fucking deal, Vince. You want to roll around and take another look at this guy."

"And do what? Jack him up for an open container and ask him if he shot a cop?"

"What about the kid? The kid said he saw his brother do it. That's a positive ID that's tough to disqualify."

Alvarez couldn't explain why the kid had done what he had. It was the weight of his testimony that tipped the scales. There was no coming back from that. Alvarez knew it and he suspected the kid knew it too."

"Maybe the kid was wrong."

• • •

Oscar Flores was trying to adjust to his new life. After the reward money came in, he and his mother moved to nearby Vallejo. It was two toll bridges away from

San Francisco, but close enough if he felt like coming back for a game he could.

Vallejo had seen better days. Lack of funds to bolster the infrastructure or pay for city services had run the town down during the past decade. Not enough police and schools that were understaffed welcomed Ria and Oscar to their new home. They bought an old tract house built in the seventies. There were plumbing problems and a little dry rot, but it was bigger than any other place they'd lived.

The reward money went quickly. There was the down payment on the house, then the hidden expenses a kid like Oscar never considered: closing costs and taxes and homeowners insurance. It was a crash course on growing up. If they were going to make it, they'd need extra income. Ria found a job right away at another salon, but the pay wasn't as good and the hours not as convenient. Their struggle was nothing the two of them couldn't handle, Oscar thought. As soon as the school year ended, he'd find himself a job and help out with the daily expenses. He'd soon be the man his mother always hoped he'd be.

By themselves, the two of them were slow to unpack. Most of what they'd brought from their apartment in the city sat undisturbed in the garage. Oscar often went out to look at it. It amazed him. The sum total of their lives fit neatly in to one quarter of the garage. A blue plastic tarp lay over their belongings.

One overcast afternoon, Oscar had returned from school and found himself restless. He walked into the garage, flipped on the light, and peeled back the tarp. There were boxes and plastic bins, laundry baskets and heavy duty garbage bags of unwashed clothes. It sat like an unorganized time capsule from a place no one wanted to remember.

Oscar reached into one of the laundry baskets and pulled a grey duffle bag that Ramon used to fill with dirty clothes. Along the garage door were some sandbags lined across the bottom to protect from rainwater that seemed to sneak in every time there was a storm. Oscar opened up the duffel bag and placed two of the small sandbags in the bottom. He then began to stuff old towels and other rags on top of the sandbags. He packed it tight, pausing every now and then to press down on its contents with his foot. When he was done and the bag felt good and solid, he threaded a rope through the metal rungs at the top of the bag. After setting up an aluminum stepladder, he climbed its rungs, then hoisted the heavy duffel by the rope over the rafters. It hung there, swaying gently like an old drunk.

Oscar climbed down and faced off with the bag. He gave it a solid punch with his right hand. Low and on the side, where he thought a man's kidneys might be. He peppered it with a few lefts, then some quick combinations. Gradually he built up some speed, some vigor, and soon he was flushed and sweating from punching the bag. He didn't stop. He kept hitting and hitting until his knuckles started to sting. They were skinned and tiny beads of blood crowned each one. Soon the bag itself was tattooed with spots of Oscar's blood. He kept punching. Harder and harder. He punched until he'd completely winded himself. He doubled over and tried to suck air into his lungs. When he straightened back up, he drew a folding pocketknife from back pocket. He clicked it into place and went at the bag, stabbing it with his right hand while hugging it with his left. He stabbed and stabbed into the bag. He stabbed until the fabric inside the bag began to hang out. He stood back for a moment, looked at Ramon's bag hanging lifeless from the rafters, then he started stabbing again. He kept at it until he could stab no more.

Exhausted, he fell back to the floor, spent and silent. Clutching the knife, he pulled his knees up close to his chin and stayed sitting on the cool garage cement. He'd received no relief from attacking the bag, no satisfaction.

Oscar thought he heard something on the other side of the garage door. The light near the bottom was blocked by the rest of the sandbags, so there was no way to tell if someone was out there. But, there was sound. The light scraping of shoes against the pavement. Someone was pacing back and forth. Oscar waited motionless, hoping whoever it was would go away.

If the noise were a delivery, a mailman, or even those nicely dressed men with religious pamphlets in their hands, they would've rang the bell. A metallic-sounding ping-pong that Oscar rarely heard since they moved in. Since the moment Oscar walked out of the San Francisco Hall of Justice, reporters hounded him for a comment, but never in their new Vallejo home.

Before Oscar even raised himself from the floor, the doorbell rang. Once more as he hurried to the front door to see who it was. Oscar didn't look through the peephole, their apartment door in the city never had one, so he didn't think to use it. He held the knife down at his side, opened the door a crack, and saw Salty's face.

With the heel of his hand, Salty shoved the door open the rest of the way.

"What's up, you piece of shit?"

It was the closest thing to a nickname Ramon had ever called him. It made Oscar cringe just to hear it.

"What do you want?"

"What'd you mean, what do I want?" Salty pushed past Oscar and into the house. "I wanna talk to you. I haven't seen you in months. Is this the way to treat an old friend?"

Salty walked to the middle of the living room and

spun around, treating the space as though it were opulent, not dingy and sparse like it was. But to Salty, maybe it was a palace. Oscar had never seen where he lived.

"Where's your mother?"

Oscar knew he shouldn't answer, shouldn't engage Salty, but he didn't see any point in lying. "She's not home. She's at work."

"Work? You made her get a job? With all the money you got? Me? I'd treat my mother like a queen."

"We don't have any money."

"No? That's not what I heard. I know what you got for what you did to Ramon. A great big check." Salty wagged a finger at him, taunting, mocking. "That's why you did it, right? That's why you sent your brother away? For the money?"

Oscar didn't say anything. He felt sick. Salty knew. Why wouldn't Salty know? He's Ramon's best friend. A strange metallic taste formed in Oscar's mouth and the room tilted a little.

"That's right," Salty slurred. "Ramon told me everything. I know all about you and your big brother." Salty glared at Oscar, a reptilian grin bent his wet lips into a cruel curve.

"Go home, Salty."

"Home? I ain't got one, thanks to you. My old man kicked me out after I came home drunk from mourning my lost friend. Said I could go room with Ramon in *la pinta*. Said I was no different from him."

"That's not my fault," Oscar said.

Salty ignored him and went on, "That's okay, he's an asshole. He don't know Ramon didn't do nothing" Salty let that one hang on the air a moment before going on. "That's why I thought I'd come over here, to my extended family. Maybe stay with them a while. Live the good life, for a change."

"You gotta go, Salty. My mom's gonna be here any minute."

Salty's tone shifted. He began to snarl and hiss. "I know what you did, you fucking piece of shit. I know you fucked up Ramon on purpose. He didn't shoot that cop and you know it. You knew it all along. You fucking sent your own brother away. You think you can do that shit and nothing's gonna happen? You're fuckin' wrong. Dead fuckin' wrong."

Oscar went cold, a chill ran over his skin and he felt each individual hair raise up on his arms and neck. He remembered the pocket knife still clutched in his right hand. He squeezed the handle so tight it barely seemed like the weapon was there at all.

"That's right. I know your secret. I know why you did it, too. So you owe me, Oscar. And you're gonna keep on owing me."

Oscar couldn't tell if Salty was drunk, or high, or

what, but he noticed him swaying a little. His eyes looked unfocused.

"You should make me a sandwich or somethin', punk. You got any beer here?"

"You gotta go, Salty. I mean it." Oscar kept the knife down at his side, hugging the seam of his pants.

"What're you gonna do? Call the cops on me?" Salty giggled. "Oh yeah, that's right, you probably will." He paused to look around his surroundings as though he'd just noticed he was inside the house. "How about that beer, bitch? You fetching it, or what?"

"You can't have nothing, Salty. You gotta go. Right now."

"Or what?" Salty stepped forward and Oscar could smell the liquor on his breath. "You gonna fight me?" He stepped a bit closer. "You gonna try to put me down?"

Oscar was backed up against a wall now. Salty's hot breath was blowing in his face.

Salty reached up with both hands and grabbed Oscar by the throat. "Maybe you want to give me some of that sweet stuff. You know, like the shit you did for your brother…"

Oscar raised the knife from his side and plunged it into Salty, right under his left armpit. Salty's eyes lit up with surprise and Oscar realized he hadn't seen the knife. He felt Salty's grip tighten for a moment and then slowly go slack. They stood there for several seconds, eye to eye, only inches between their faces. Then Salty's hands fell away from Oscar's neck entirely and he collapsed to the floor.

Oscar stood over Salty's body and watched him bleed out onto the floor. Bright arterial blood seeped onto the linoleum tiles, growing into a puddle, reaching all the way to the rug. Oscar was surprised at how bright the blood was. Nothing like that day, nothing like the dark stream in the gutter on Capp Street.

ACKNOWLEDGMENTS

First off, I'd like to thank my wife, Cheryl, and my kids, Logan, Dane, and Lula, for their patience with my obsessions and for being stalwart Giants fans. And to Ron Earl Phillips at Shotgun Honey Books for his tolerance of my haphazard approach to writing and for taking a chance on the book. Also, thanks to Joe Clifford and Bob Pitts for their insight and input. And lastly, thanks to Bryan Stow, whose tragic story was the impetus for this book.

Tom Pitts received his education on the streets of San Francisco. He remains there, working, writing, and trying to survive. He is the author of, HUSTLE, and the novella, Piggyback.

Find links to more of his work at: TomPittsAuthor. com

ABOUT SHOTGUN HONEY BOOKS

Thank you for reading *Knuckleball* by Tom Pitts.

Shotgun Honey began as a crime genre flash fiction webzine in 2011 created as a venue for new and established writers to experiment in the confines of a mere 700 words. More than a decade later, Shotgun Honey still challenges writers with that storytelling task, but also provides opportunities to expand beyond through our book imprint and has since published anthologies, collections, novellas and novels by new and emerging authors.

We hope you have enjoyed this book. That you will share your experience, review and rate this title positively on your favorite book review sites and with your social media family and friends.

Visit ShotgunHoneyBooks.com

SHOTGUN
HONEY
FICTION WITH A KICK
shotgunhoneybooks.com